MONSTER ADOPTION SPECIAL

WINGED
SCALY
FURRY

Adoption
saves lives!

HUGSBY

Dow Phumiruk

VIKING

VIKING
An imprint of Penguin Random House LLC, New York

First published in the United States of America by Viking,
an imprint of Penguin Random House LLC, 2020

Visit us online at penguinrandomhouse.com

LIBRARY OF CONGRESS CATALOGING-IN-PUBLICATION DATA IS AVAILABLE.
ISBN 9781984835987

Manufactured in China   Set in Archer
1 3 5 7 9 10 8 6 4 2

The art for this book was created with pencil and Photoshop, including scanned watercolor textures.

For my huggable friends and family

The day Shelly brought Hugsby home, she knew he was
not like any other pet monster.
Hugsby couldn't do any fancy tricks.
He didn't roll over or fetch.
He didn't know how to whistle or blow bubbles.

But Shelly didn't care. She loved him. And he loved her . . .
MONSTER-ously so.

They played together,

laughed together,

and said "sweet dreams" to each other.

When Shelly went to school, Hugsby waited all day long for her to come home.

Sometimes he would draw pictures . . .

or bake cookies.

Sometimes he'd practice blowing bubbles.

But really he couldn't wait to do what he loved best . . . hug Shelly.

One day, Shelly announced, "Tomorrow is Pet Monster Show-and-Tell Day! You can come to school with me, Hugsby!"

Hugsby jumped up and down in excitement.

"We just need to teach you a trick or something," Shelly said.

Shelly threw a toy and asked Hugsby to fetch.

Hugsby just sat and smiled.

Shelly tried to teach
Hugsby to juggle,

but instead he almost
ate the beanbags.

He couldn't figure out how to fold a paper airplane

or do a handstand,

and he still couldn't
blow bubbles.

Finally, Shelly tried to teach Hugsby to dance . . .
but he hugged her instead.
She couldn't teach him anything!
"Oh, Hugsby," sighed Shelly.

Hugsby was tired, so Shelly tucked him in for a nap.
"I love you anyway, Hugsby," she whispered.

The next morning, Hugsby woke up early. He held Shelly's hand and skipped all the way to school.

After the school bell rang, Mrs. Peach had the children introduce their monsters, and then they all sang a Welcome, Monsters song.

Shelly thought that show-and-tell might be okay after all.

Shelly
Tommy
Celeste
Sabrina
Audrey
Madeline
Quentin
Declan
Mali
Patrick
Brandon
Kit
Mikayla
Lucas
Caden

Welcome, monsters! Welcome, monsters!
We're so happy that you're here.
Welcome, monsters! Welcome, monsters!
Let's all give a great big cheer:
Hip hip hooray
for this Super Pet Monster Day!!

Tommy went first. "Snow Guy is really big and really strong!"

Hugsby isn't big or strong, thought Shelly.

Celeste was next. She and her monster, Lottie, put on a magic show.

Hugsby doesn't know any magic tricks, thought Shelly.

"Greenie is a gymnast! He can do triple backflips!" Henry said.

Shelly gulped. Hugsby couldn't do a single flip. He couldn't even do a somersault.

There were so many kinds of monsters, and they all could do something special.

country-music
singing monster

karate monster

mime monster

cellist monster

soccer monster

invisible monster who
bakes

hula-hooping monster

ballerina monster

glow-in-the-dark fuzzy monster

tap-dancing monster

yoga monster

superhero monster

tightrope-walking monster

artist monster

Shelly was worried.
What was Hugsby good at?

Finally, it was Hugsby's turn.
Shelly mumbled.

"My monster . . . sits really still . . .
and . . . he's a good listener . . . and . . ."

"...and..."

"... he gives great hugs just when you need them!"
Shelly hugged him back.

Then Shelly couldn't believe it . . .
everyone wanted hugs from Hugsby.

Shelly didn't care if Hugsby was big or strong or could do triple flips.
She didn't care if he could blow fancy bubbles.
Hugsby gave the best hugs . . . and he gave them to everyone.

...8...9...10...